by Anna Kang illustrated by Christopher Weyant

THAT'S
(NOT) MINE

Hodder
Children's
Books

An Imprint of Hachette Children's Group

To our parents for their loving support

and for teaching us how to share.

That's (Not) Mine by Anna Kang
Illustrated by Christopher Weyant

This edition published in the UK in 2015 by Hodder Children's Books.
Originally published by Amazon Publishing.
Used with the permission of Pippin Properties, Inc. through Rights People, London.

Text copyright © Anna Kang 2015
Illustrations copyright © Christopher Weyant 2015

Hodder Children's Books
An imprint of Hachette Children's Group
Part of Hodder & Stoughton
Carmelite House
50 Victoria Embankment
London EC4Y 0DZ

The right of Anna Kang and Christopher Weyant to be identified as
the author and illustrator of this Work has been asserted by them in
accordance with the Copyright, Designs and Patents Act 1988.

A catalogue record of this book is available from the British Library.

ISBN 978 1 444 91832 8

Printed in China

An Hachette UK Company
www.hachette.co.uk

FSC
www.fsc.org

MIX
From responsible
sources
FSC® C104740

I was sitting in it before.

I'm sitting
in it now.

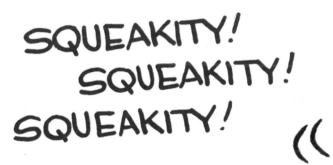

OK, just once.

FLING!